LIVY LUZ AND THE CRISPY CHEWY COSMIC COOKIES

NICOLE A. MORALES

Outskirts Press, Inc.
http://www.outskirtspress.com

ISBN: 978-1-4787-9605-3

Outskirts Press and the "OP" logo are trademarks belonging to Outskirts Press, Inc.

PRINTED IN THE UNITED STATES OF AMERICA

This Book Belongs to:

Elle Lamm

To: Elle
I hope you enjoy
this book as much
as you'll enjoy
making and eating
the delicious
cookies
—Nicole A. Morales

elcome to the Cookie Cove Bakery. My name is Livy Luz and this amazing cookie shop is owned by my Mommy and Daddy. Do you want to know a secret?

My parents are cookie-making wizards! Ok, not actual wizards, but they work some serious baking magic to come up with delicious cookie recipes, like…

Brown Cow Brookies (½ brownie, ½ chocolate chip cookie), Mornin' Shakin' Maple Bacon Cookies (They taste like breakfast!), Whirly Swirly Cranberry Walnut Spirals (Grandma's favorite) and Nu Che-Che Cookies (A mix of Nutella and Dulce de Leche. Mmmmm!)

The Cookie Cove Bakery is always filled with customers. Everyone loves my family's cookies. I love them the most! I am always Mommy and Daddy's first customer and official taste-tester of every new cookie creation.

I love getting to try all the cookies my parents come up with, but I want to be more than the shop's cookie taster. I want to be just like my parents and create an amazing cookie. Not just amazing… THE BEST COOKIE IN THE UNIVERSE!

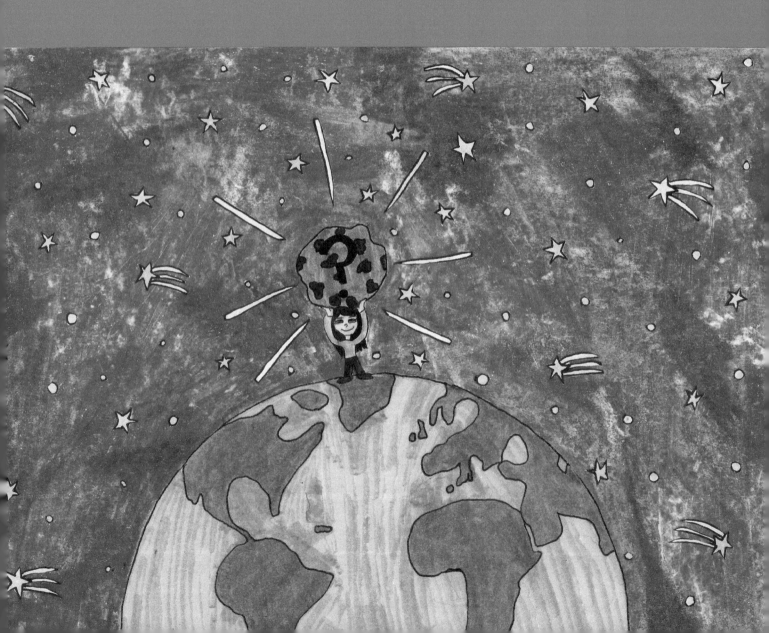

What could I do that my parents hadn't already tried? Hmmm. Well, Daddy's favorite cookies are Nutty Nutty Peanut Buttery Cookies. Mommy's favorites are Chocolate Chip Volcanoes; Chocolate lava spills out once you bite into the cookie! I thought about combining their favorites into one cookie, but I remembered they'd already done that last summer with the creation of the Volcanic Choco-nut Cookies. Creating a new cookie is going to be a challenge.

I decided to go to the experts. I asked, "Mommy, Daddy, how do you come up with all of your crazy cookie ideas?" "Well, I like to talk to many different people to find out what they like and dislike," answered Mommy. "You see, Livy Luz," said Daddy, "it's all about thinking outside of the box. Sometimes the cookies we make come out delicious and other times they are awful, but we don't give up. We keep trying until we find a winner!" I thanked them for their advice and set off on my mission. I now had the steps to follow to get my cookie process in motion.

Step 1: Talk.

I talked to the people I know from my neighborhood. Mr. Parcel, the mailman, said he loves any cookies that are sweet. Mrs. Flowers, my neighbor, told me that she adores chocolate cookies.

I also talked to my teacher and my friend. My teacher, Miss Classman said she loves a sweet cookie with a hint of salty. My friend, Crispin, told me he prefers potato chips. Go figure!

1 cup = 8 oz.
3 tsp = 1 tbsp
1 gallon = 4 quarts

TALK

Step 2: Think.

Ok, Daddy had told me to think outside of the box. What if I mix sweet and salty just like my teacher said? And, what if I did that by using ingredients that are not usually found in a cookie recipe? Yes!

Step 3: Try.

I decided to start with a basic chocolate chip cookie recipe because Mommy always says, "A classic never goes out of style." Next, I added peanut butter chips, for Daddy. That was the easy part. Now what?

Some of the people I had spoken to said they loved sweet, chocolatey cookies. The idea came to me in a flash! I grabbed some chocolate sandwich cookies, placed them in a bag and crushed them up. Into the mixing bowl they went.

Next, it was time to add something salty. Well, the saltiest snack I could think of was pretzels. I crumbled those up and poured them in.

The cookie was almost perfect, but I wanted to add something that was totally different from normal cookie ingredients. I thought and thought, and I thought some more. Finally, I remembered that Crispin had said he preferred potato chips over cookies. That was it! I added potato chips to my cookie dough.

I mixed everything together and began spooning the dough onto a cookie sheet. Mommy put the cookie sheet in the oven for me and we waited for them to bake. It didn't take long for the delicious smell to fill the kitchen. I tried to be patient, but it felt like the cookies were taking FOREVER to bake!

DING! The timer rang out, signaling that the cookies were done. Daddy took them out of the oven and placed them on the cooling rack.

When the cookies had finally cooled, it was time to taste them. I felt nervous. What if they didn't taste yummy? What if people thought they were gross? What if I had failed and would never be as good as my parents?

Good or bad, it was time for the ultimate taste test. I took my first bite... AMAZING! They were the most delicious cookies I had ever eaten. I immediately asked Mommy and Daddy to try them. They loved them. The cookies were a success. I was a success!

"Livy Luz, we are so proud of you for creating this wonderful cookie and, especially, for being brave enough to try," cried Mommy. Daddy hugged me and said, "We are going to add your cookie to the shop's menu!" I was so excited. "Before we can put it on the menu," Daddy said, "You need to give it a name and, remember, a cookie so out-of-this-world deserves an out-of-this-world name." Hmmm. It was kind of crunchy and a bit chewy and, of course, out-of-this-world. What would be the perfect name for my awesome cookie? I didn't have to think for long.

Crunchy Chewy Cosmic Cookies!

Crunchy Chewy Cosmic Cookies

makes 2 dozen cookies

¾ cup brown sugar

¾ cup granulated sugar

2 ½ sticks butter (softened)

1 teaspoon baking soda

½ cup potato chips (broken into small pieces)

½ cup salted pretzels (broken into small pieces)

½ cup chocolate sandwich cookies (crush into crumbs)

3 eggs

2 teaspoons vanilla extract

3 cups all-purpose flour

½ teaspoon salt

1 ½ cups chocolate chips

½ cup peanut butter chips

- Preheat the oven to 325° F.
- In a large bowl, mix brown sugar with granulated sugar.
- Add the butter and beat at low speed.
- Beat in the eggs and vanilla.
- Add the flour, baking soda and salt. Mix.
- Add the chocolate sandwich cookie crumbs. Mix.
- Add the chocolate chips and the peanut butter chips. Mix.
- Beat in the pretzels and potato chips.
- Spoon 2 tablespoons of dough onto ungreased cookie sheet, spaced about 2 inches apart.
- Bake for 15 – 20 minutes, until edges have set and are slightly browned. Bake longer for a crunchier cookie.
- Remove from oven and leave them on the cookie sheet for 5 minutes.
- Move them to a wire rack to cool completely.

Hint: Use a non-stick whoopie pie pan for fluffier cookies!

CPSIA information can be obtained
at www.ICGtesting.com
Printed in the USA
BVHW020950200519
548788BV00003B/45/P

9781478796053